亲爱的爸爸妈妈们：

在阅读这本书之前，您可以让您的孩子先在左侧的横线上写下自己的名字——这可能成为他（她）完完整整读完的第一本书，也因此成为真正意义上第一本属于他（她）自己的书。

作为美国最知名的儿童启蒙阅读丛书"I Can Read!"中的一册，它专为刚开始阅读起步的孩子量身打造，具有用词简单、句子简短、适当重复，以及注重语言的韵律和节奏等特点。这些特点非常有助于孩子对语言的学习，不论是学习母语，还是学习作为第二语言的英语。

故事的主角是鼎鼎大名的贝贝熊一家，这一风靡美国近半个世纪的形象对孩子具有天然的亲和力，很多跟贝贝熊有关的故事都为孩子所津津乐道。作为双语读物，它不但能引导孩子独立捧起书本，去了解书中有趣的情节，还能做到真正从兴趣出发，让孩子领略到英语学习的乐趣。

就从贝贝熊开始，让您的孩子爱上阅读，帮助他们开启自己的双语阅读之旅吧！

D1529548

图书在版编目（CIP）数据

过夜的小客人：汉英对照 / （美）博丹(Berenstain,J.)，（美）博丹(Berenstain,M.)
著；姚雁青译. —乌鲁木齐：新疆青少年出版社，2013.1
（贝贝熊系列丛书）

ISBN 978-7-5515-2740-8

Ⅰ.①过… Ⅱ.①博… ②博… ③姚… Ⅲ.①英语－汉语－对照读物②儿童故
事－美国－现代 Ⅳ.①H319.4：Ⅰ

中国版本图书馆CIP数据核字(2012)第273209号

版权登记：图字 29-2012-24

The Berenstain Bears' Sleepover
copyright©2009 by Berenstain Bears, Inc.
This edition arranged with Sterling Lord Literistic, Inc.
through Andrew Nurnberg Associates International Limited

贝贝熊系列丛书
过夜的小客人

（美）简·博丹 麦克·博丹 绘著 Jan & Mike Berenstain 姚雁青 译

出版人	徐 江		策 划	许国萍
责任编辑	贺艳华		美术编辑	查 璇 刘小珍
法律顾问	钟 麟 13201203567（新疆国法律师事务所）			

新疆青少年出版社
（地址：乌鲁木齐市北京北路29号 邮编：830012）
Http://www.qingshao.net　E-mail：QSbeijing@hotmail.com

印 刷	北京时尚印佳彩色印刷有限公司		经 销	全国新华书店
开 本	787mm×1092mm 1/16		印 张	2
版 次	2013年1月第1版		印 次	2013年1月第1次印刷
印 数	1-10000册		定 价	9.00元
标准书号	ISBN 978-7-5515-2740-8			

制售盗版必究 举报查实奖励:0991-7833932　版权保护办公室举报电话：0991-7833927
销售热线:010-84853493 84851485　如有印刷装订质量问题 印刷厂负责掉换

The Berenstain Bears'

I Can Read!

贝贝熊系列丛书
双语阅读

SLEEPOVER
过夜的小客人

(美) 简·博丹 麦克·博丹 绘著
Jan & Mike Berenstain

姚雁青 译

CHISO SINCE 1956 新疆青少年出版社

Sister and Brother Bear were having a sleepover.
Lizzy and Barry Bruin were
Sister's and Brother's best friends.
They were going to spend the night.

这一天，小熊妹妹和小熊哥哥要举办"熬夜派对"。
他们最要好的朋友，布鲁因家的两个小熊——丽兹和巴里，
要来家里过夜。

Lizzy and Barry's parents brought them
to the Bears' tree house.
"I hope Lizzy and Barry sleep well
tonight," said Mrs. Bruin.
"We'll make sure they don't stay up
too late," said Mama Bear.

丽兹和巴里的爸爸妈妈把他们送到贝贝熊家的树屋。
"我希望丽兹和巴里今晚能睡个好觉。"布鲁因太太说。
"我们不会让他们睡得太晚。"熊妈妈保证。

Lizzy and Barry put their things
in Sister and Brother's room.
Then they all had dinner.

丽兹和巴里把他们的东西放到小熊妹妹和小熊哥哥的房间里。
然后，他们一起吃晚饭。

After dinner the cubs played
a game of Bearopoly.
Lizzy was winning, and soon owned
most of the tree houses.
The other cubs gave up.

吃完晚饭，小熊们一起玩小熊飞行棋。
丽兹赢了，她把大家所有的树屋棋子都吃掉了。
其他的小熊只能认输。

Next, they watched a movie.

It was about a wizard.

The wizard had a cape.

It gave him magical powers!

下完棋，他们一起看电影。

电影讲了一个巫师的故事。

这位巫师有件斗篷，能赋予他神奇的魔力！

The cubs decided to put on
their own magic show.
They got costumes out of the attic.
The audience was Mama, Papa, and Honey.

小熊们决定上演自己的魔法秀。
他们从阁楼里翻出表演用的服装，
请熊爸爸、熊妈妈和熊宝宝当观众。

The show went well until Barry tripped
on his magic cape.
He knocked over Brother, Sister, and Lizzy!
They laughed and laughed.
"The show is over!" said Mama.
"Time for bed."

表演进行得非常顺利，可突然间，巴里被他的魔法斗篷绊倒了。
他还撞倒了小熊哥哥、小熊妹妹和丽兹！
大家笑啊，笑啊。
　"魔法秀到此结束！"熊妈妈宣布，"该上床睡觉啦。"

The cubs put on their pajamas,
washed up, and brushed their teeth.
Mama and Papa read them
a bedtime story and tucked them in.

小熊们换上睡衣，然后洗脸、刷牙。
熊爸爸和熊妈妈给他们讲了睡前故事，然后帮他们盖好了被子。

"Goodnight, everyone," said Mama,
turning out the lights.

"宝贝们，晚安！"熊妈妈说着，关上了灯。

Mama and Papa went to bed
and were soon asleep.
But the cubs were not at all sleepy.
Brother got out his flashlight.
"Let's tell spooky stories!" he said.

熊爸爸和熊妈妈上床睡觉，他们很快就睡着了。
但是小熊们一点儿都不困。
小熊哥哥翻出手电筒，提议道："我们来讲鬼故事吧！"

Mama woke up.
She thought she heard something.
She woke Papa and they went
to the cubs' room.

熊妈妈惊醒了，她觉得自己听到了一些动静。
她叫醒熊爸爸，和他一起来到小熊们的房间。

Sister and Lizzy were hiding under the covers.
Brother and Barry seemed to be sleeping.

小熊妹妹和丽兹躲在被子底下。
小熊哥哥和巴里在装睡。

"What is going on here?" asked Papa.
"Brother was telling a spooky story,"
said Sister,
"and Lizzy got scared and yelled."

"这儿怎么了？"熊爸爸问。
"哥哥讲了一个鬼故事，丽兹吓坏了，喊了一声。"小熊妹妹回答。

"That's enough spooky stories," said Mama.
"Now everyone go to sleep!"

"鬼故事到此为止吧。"熊妈妈说,"现在,大家都赶快睡觉!"

Mama and Papa went back to bed.

Mama heard something again.

She woke Papa and they went downstairs.

熊妈妈和熊爸爸回到床上。

熊妈妈又听到了动静，

她叫醒熊爸爸，和他一起下了楼。

They found the cubs in the kitchen
eating snacks.
"It is too late for snacks," Mama said.
"Back to bed!"

他们发现小熊们正在厨房里吃夜宵。
　"现在吃东西有点儿太晚了，" 熊妈妈说，"快回去睡觉！"

Mama and Papa went back to bed again.
But Mama heard a sound in the bathroom.
She woke Papa.

熊妈妈和熊爸爸又回到床上。
很快，熊妈妈听到浴室里传来一声响动。
她连忙叫醒熊爸爸。

They found Sister and Lizzy
putting on Mama's lipstick.
Brother and Barry were covered in
Papa's shaving cream.
"That's enough of that!" said Mama.
"Back to bed!"

他们看到，小熊妹妹和丽兹正往嘴唇上抹熊妈妈的口红，
小熊哥哥和巴里的脸上涂满了熊爸爸的剃须膏。

"你们闹够了吧！"熊妈妈有点儿火了，"都回去睡觉！"

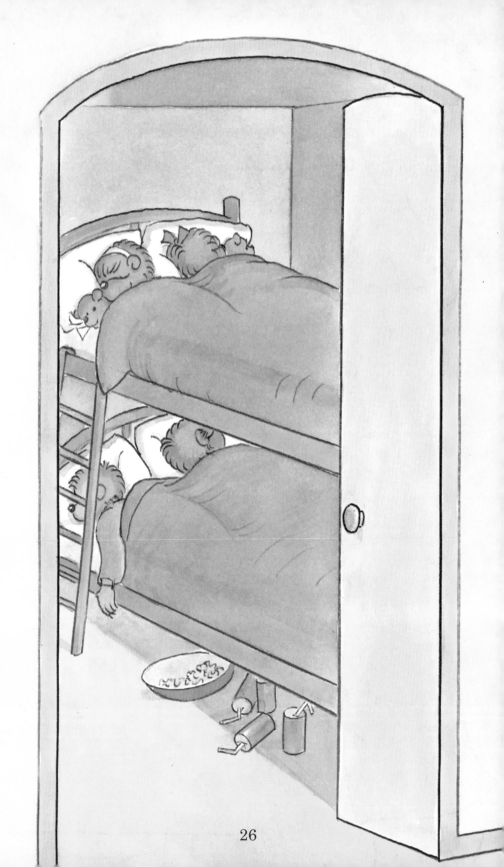

Now the cubs were worn out.

They went right to sleep.

Mama and Papa sat outside

the cubs' room all night.

They did not get much sleep.

这时，小熊们已经玩得筋疲力尽了，

他们倒在床上，很快就睡着了。

熊妈妈和熊爸爸在小熊们的房间外坐了整整一夜，

几乎没有合眼。

The next morning the cubs slept late.

第二天早上，小熊们睡了个大大的懒觉。

At eleven o'clock, Mr. and Mrs. Bruin
came to pick up Lizzy and Barry.
"I was so worried about them!" said Mrs. Bruin.
"I didn't sleep a wink all night!"
"Neither did we," said Papa,
his eyes closing.

11点钟，布鲁因先生和布鲁因太太来接丽兹和巴里。
"我真担心这两个小家伙！"布鲁因太太说，"我一整夜都没睡着觉！"
"我们也一样啊！"熊爸爸叹了口气说。
他连眼皮都抬不起来了。

After Lizzy and Barry went home,
Mama and Papa sat down on the sofa.
They were soon asleep.

丽兹和巴里走了之后，
熊爸爸和熊妈妈在沙发上坐下来。
他们困极了，很快就睡着了。

It was Mama and Papa's turn for a sleepover!

这回，轮到熊爸爸和熊妈妈当熬夜派对的客人啦！